Quiet Please!

READ MORE ADVENTURES ABOUT TWIG AND TURTLE!

TWiG AND TURTLE

Quiet
Please!

Jennifer Richard Jacobson

Illustrated by Paula Franco

PIXEL✚INK

For Dian, Laya, and Kerry

PIXEL✚INK

Text copyright © 2020 by Jennifer Richard Jacobson
Illustrations copyright © 2020 by TGM Development Corp.
Pixel+Ink is a division of TGM Development Corp.
Printed and bound in November 2020 at Maple Press, York, PA, U.S.A.
Cover and interior design by Georgia Morrissey
www.pixelandinkbooks.com
Library of Congress Control Number: 2020940461
Hardcover ISBN 978-1-64595-044-8
Paperback ISBN 978-1-64595-045-5
eBook ISBN 978-1-64595-063-9
First Edition
1 3 5 7 9 10 8 6 4 2

CHAPTER 1

SMACK!

I look up from my book for the umpteenth time. "Turtle, can't you go somewhere else and do that?" I ask. I'm sitting on the couch and she's right beside me, chomping on a giant wad of gum and practicing blowing bubbles.

"I can't!" she says. "Mom won't let me chew gum in the loft."

True. The last time Turtle chewed gum in our loft, it stuck our sleeping bags together.

"Then at least sit on a stool," I say.

The stools are not much farther away from me. My family lives in a tiny house, which basically means one big room with two lofts overhead. The only room in the house that has a door is the bathroom.

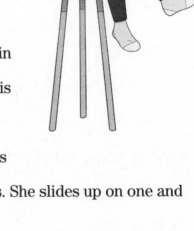

Turtle gets up and takes the five steps to the stools. She slides up on one and resumes her practicing.

SMACK!

It is so annoying. All mouth noises are annoying. The only time I can stand mouth noises is when I'm eating too. Then I don't notice them.

2

BAM!

That's Dad jumping down from my parents' loft.

"I have to lose weight," he says as he slides next to me on the couch.

"*I* have to keep reading," I tell him.

"What are you reading now?" he asks, probably just to get me riled.

I place my finger on the page so I won't lose my place and show him the cover: *Mystery of the Haunted Barn.*

"That looks scary!" he says. "Is it?"

"Not really," I tell him. "But this series is easy to read, so I can keep up my stamina!" Our school is having a read-a-thon. The class that reads the most hours gets to go bowling right in the middle of a school day!

And my class is counting on me. As my friend David said, "Twig McKay"—that's me—"is the most voracious reader I know." I suppose that might be true. I do gobble up books.

"How many hours have you read?" Turtle asks, pulling the gum mass out of her mouth and leaving it on the counter.

4

"Seventy-three," I say. "And there's only one week left."

I turn back to the story. I'm reading about some kids who hear a ghost going, "*Whoooo.*" Why do ghosts always make that sound in books? Ghosts can talk, right? Why don't they say something like "I'm warning you to leave now or I'll grab you with my ghostly fingers!" That would be sooooo much scarier.

Dad reaches for the TV remote. Turtle immediately jumps down and says, "Let's do *Dance Like a Flamingo!*"

"Not now," I say. "I'm trying to read!"

"You can go up to the loft," Turtle says.

Dad looks at me. "I'd move the TV if I could."

"But I can still hear you!"

"You can wear the headphones up there," Dad

5

says, reaching for our only pair.

"But I can still feel the jumping." (The whole house actually wobbles. It's not easy to concentrate when you're bouncing.)

"Go to the studio," Turtle says.

My parents have a studio next door in the back of Sudsy's Laundromat. Mom is there now. She's a photographer and even though it's Sunday, she has a deadline. (That means she has to send very artsy photos by the end of the day.) When Mom or Dad have deadlines, no one else is allowed in the studio. I remind Turtle of that. And the fact that it's too cold to sit in one place outside—or in the car—and read.

"Can't you guys dance later?" I ask.

"But you're *always* reading!" Turtle says.

I guess she's right. Normally, I read a lot. This past week, I've been reading every single minute I can.

I huff and get up from my seat. I grab a pillow and take it with me into the bathroom. At least I can get some peace and quiet in there. I'll probably still feel the bouncing, but I won't worry that it will cause me to come crashing down seven feet.

I pull the pocket door shut and look for a place to sit. It's not easy. My friend Angela's house has three bathrooms and they're all ginormous! In her parents' bathroom, there's a tub and a shower—and they're separate from one another! I could lie down in the middle of her guest bathroom with my arms and legs flapping like a snow angel and not touch anything.

Our bathroom is tiny just like the rest of the house. I can sit on the toilet and brush my teeth over the sink. We have a combination tub and shower, but the tub isn't a normal size. It's square, and I need to pull my knees into my chest to take a bath.

7

But it might work for reading.

I place the pillow at one end, step into the tub, and pull the curtain shut to make a cool reading fort. Then I place my feet up the opposite wall.

I can still hear faint music, but it's sort of like reading at the beach, where you can hear noise, but it doesn't interrupt your reading.

Back to the story:

Whoooooo!

Diego and Amira race into the old barn and slide the door shut.

The ghostly sound follows them.

It gets louder . . .

And louder . . .

I stop reading.

I hear a sound. It's coming closer. Is it a ghost? A hand reaches behind the curtain and . . . turns on the shower! *ACK!!!*

"Mom!" I yell. "What are you doing?!"

CHAPTER 2

"What are you doing in the shower?" Mom asks, handing me a towel to dry off my head and face.

"Trying to find a quiet place to read," I say. My clothes are soaked. And the library book is soaked too! I set it on the edge of the sink and use the towel to dry it off as best I can.

Mom is eager to take a shower, so I grab some dry clothes from my drawer. Then I sneak past Dad and Turtle, who are in a laughing heap on the couch, and climb the stairs to our loft.

I'd grabbed my Determined Squirrel T-shirt. Dad, who draws comics for a living, created him. The shirt's perfect for today, because even though I have a soccer game this afternoon, I am determined to read for at least three hours!

Because the ceiling is so low, it's impossible for me to stand up straight, so most of my time in the loft is spent on my bed. Turtle and I share a mattress, but we each have our own sleeping bag. Mine's closest to the railing, so I can peak down to the big room whenever I want.

At this very moment, I can see Turtle grabbing her jacket and racing out the front door onto the porch. It's windy, and the wind gusts into the house and makes me shiver.

I don't want to get my sleeping bag wet, so I stand with my shoulders and head bent over and try to slip off my wet jeans. Now *I'm* the one doing a weird flamingo dance, trying to balance on one leg and then the other. When I've finally pulled the pants off (yuck!), I kneel down and pull off the rest of my clothes.

Even though Turtle is outside, her voice comes floating up to me. I can hear her talking to someone and I wonder if it's Cara from Cara's Carrots. Cara's food truck is parked right next door to our house. She often gives us yummy samples like little fried carrots dipped in creamy dressing or chocolate-covered carrots.

The thought of samples makes me hungry. Maybe if I hurry, I can catch them.

I've just pulled off my wet shirt (Why do wet clothes stick to skin?) when the front door opens again and I hear Turtle say, "This door leads right into our kitchen."

ACK! Turtle must be giving another one of her house tours! I'm in full view and I'm practically naked. I quick wiggle into my sleeping bag.

"We don't have a dishwasher, but we do have a full-sized refrigerator complete with an icemaker!"

My sister gives tours about once a week. People are really curious about tiny houses. And because ours is right on Main Street in Happy Trails, they don't think of it as a real house. They think it's a place that anyone can visit anytime.

Once someone came right up to the window in our door and peered inside. That was scarier than icy ghost fingers.

Turtle gives so many tours, I sometimes wonder if she just asks folks passing by if they want to see inside.

I peer through the railing. Behind Turtle is a woman with a cute baby in her arms.

"Hello," says Dad, holding out his hand. He doesn't mind it when Turtle gives tours. He loves showing folks all the sneaky places we hide things—like our puzzles behind the folding table and our shoes in the cupboards beneath the stairs.

"And you should see where we keep our toys," Turtle says as she leads them up the loft stairs.

No! I slide down deeper into the bag.

"Oh, hello!" says the woman, bending over from the top of the stairs and peering into our loft. "I hope we're not waking you."

I smile and shake my head.

The baby wants to get out of her mother's arms. She reaches down for me to take her.

I can't. "I was just putting my clothes on," I say.

16

"Oh, I'm sorry!" the woman says.

"That's okay!" Turtle says, even though it's a hundred percent not!

I poke back into my sleeping bag and slip my dry shirt over my head. When I pop out again, the woman and her baby are back downstairs.

Sometimes I like tours, but mostly they make me grouchy.

It's not that I don't like meeting people.

I do.

It's not that I don't like living in a tiny house.

I do.

But in moments like these, when I'm a practically naked girl trapped in my sleeping bag, I feel like shouting, "Privacy please!"

CHAPTER
3

That afternoon, I race to my team's bleacher on the side of the soccer field with my new cleats in hand. I'm one of the last kids to get them and I can't wait to show them off.

The tiny house rule is that we can each have two pairs of shoes. But Grandma sent them anyway saying, "Cleats are sporting equipment."

I like how my grandma thinks. When I reminded my parents that we keep the rest of my soccer gear in the trunk of our little car, and not in the house,

19

they gave in and let me
keep the cleats.

My cleats aren't
brandy new. Someone
owned them before
me. I imagine that the
former owner was an
amazing soccer player and that some of their foot
magic is still in these cleats.

While Mom and Dad and Turtle situate them-
selves on the sidelines, I race to the bench. David is
already there. I wait for him to notice my cleats. But
he doesn't.

"How many hours have you read this weekend?"
he asks.

He's probably the only kid in our class more
obsessed with winning the read-a-thon than I am.

"Four," I tell him. "But I want to get at least two more hours in before the night is over."

Just then, Matteo, another kid from my class, comes running up. "I've read seven hours this week-end so far!" he says. I've never seen him smile so big.

"Seven?" I say, slipping on my cleats and tightening my laces. "How did you do that? It sounds like you've done nothing but read."

If possible, his smile gets bigger. "My parents are away, and my babysitter is so thrilled that all I want to do is read."

"Excellent!" says David, recording Matteo's hours in his notebook. He's our official class record keeper.

I'm psyched . . . sort of. Matteo is helping us all to win the read-a-thon. But I've gotten used to having more hours than everyone else. I hate knowing that I'm losing my top-reader shininess.

Coach Ruby calls us over and gives us our starting
positions. I've played soccer since I was four and
can handle the ball fairly well, so I'm usually a midfielder. But not today. Today I'm goalkeeper! Cool!
I've never been goalkeeper before. Knowing Coach
Ruby has faith in me makes me feel a little better.

She hands me the big gloves and makes sure my
shin pads are tight enough. I slip a long-sleeved jersey

over my own shirt and pop in my mouth guard. Then I head onto the field.

I've only been keeper once before and that was before we moved to Happy Trails. I race to the net. Then I look for my family sitting on the grass and wave.

Mom gives me a "Look at you!" face.

I try to remember everything I've learned. I find my stable position and practice shuffling side to side.

A coin is tossed. Our team gets the ball first. Piper, our star scorer, kicks it down the field.

Be fearless, I tell myself. *Go after every shot.*

We have a strong offensive team today, so for the longest time, all of the play is at the other end of the field.

Come on, I think. *Bring it here.*

Their midfielder gets the ball and moves past

center, but then Piper intercepts and again all the action moves away from me.

I take a deep breath. The air smells like warm grass and dried leaves. People who've lived in Happy Trails longer than we have tell us that it often snows in the fall. That hasn't happened yet. I look up at the clouds to see if today might be the day.

I doubt it. There's not a cloud in the sky.

"Be ready, goalkeeper!" someone shouts from the sidelines.

I look to see the red jerseys of the other team coming straight at me.

Be fearless, I tell myself.

Go for every shot.

A tall forward takes a moment to get the ball under control, and then shoots!

The ball hooks toward the far right of the net and

I dive for it, just like Coach Ruby taught us. My

fingers make contact with the ball and push it away.

Yes!

Save!

I MADE A SAVE!

The crowd cheers.

So cool! I feel like taking a little bow.

I stand at the ready. But again, the action is at the other end of the pitch.

Next time I hope to catch the ball. I remember Coach telling us that it's better to roll the ball back to a teammate than throw it. (It's easier for the teammate to get it under control.)

I do a couple of imaginary rolls.

Which remind me of bowling.

I've only been bowling once. I wonder if the bowling alley we'll go to will have bumpers to prevent gutter balls. I hate gutter balls.

Of course, our class will only go bowling *if* we win the read-a-thon.

How many hours have the other third- and fourth-grade classes clocked, I wonder.

"Twig!" It's Dad's voice. "Breakaway!"

One player has left the pack and is dribbling the

ball directly toward me. . . .

I pull myself back into position. . . .

Waaap! The forward gives the ball a solid kick toward the goal.

I throw myself at it, but I'm too late.

The crowd cheers, but this time it's not for me.

First goal for the other team.

Ack! Being goalkeeper and letting a ball get past you is worse than gutter balls!

I tell myself to focus. To keep my eye on the ball at all times. But all I can think about is missing that last one. Did I keep my head up? Was I too far to the right? Why wasn't I quick enough?

Matteo dribbles down the field, but an opposing player intercepts the ball and races toward me.

I'm ready!

He kicks, and I lunge. The ball misses the goal.

Instead it rolls out of bounds.

Phew!

I'm beginning to feel like soccer is a lot like bowling, and I'm the human pin!

"Good job, Twig!" Mom yells even though I didn't really do anything.

"Get ready, goalkeeper!" another parent calls from the sidelines. "They're coming at you again!"

Suddenly, I feel very watched. More watched than when I'm sitting on the front porch of our tiny house. I feel like I'm a mouse in a cage. Only, I don't know if I'm a cute little mouse or food for a pet snake.

The play comes down to my end of the field. An opposing player takes a shot.

It bounces off David's chest.

The opposing player gets control of the ball again.

She kicks.

Matteo intercepts.

The opposing player steals
it back and shoots!

I lunge!

The ball goes over
my head.

I swear I can hear
people on the sidelines groan.

After a few more minutes,
Coach Ruby has Mia swap places with me.

I sit on the bench.

"Well done, Twig," she says to me.

Here's how you know that someone is just saying something to make you feel better:

• They don't look you in the eye or pat you on
the shoulder.

• They don't say something specific like: You had great focus!

• They say the very same thing to the other kids who were on the field too.

After a few minutes, Coach Ruby puts me back in the game as a midfielder. I've lost my excitement. I keep dreaming of goalkeeping—of catching the ball.

If only I hadn't been so quick to dive.

If only I'd thrown my whole body at it.

If only I'd been more fearless.

The referee blows his whistle.

The game ends.

We lose. Two to nothing.

CHAPTER 4

Thankfully, Bo, our school reading dog, comes
to stay overnight at our house. He used to live with
my grandma (and me too, sort of). When our school
custodian, Mr. Kim (who adopted Bo), has to be out
of town, or whenever we get lonely for our Great
Dane, Bo comes to sleep with us. Tonight, Mr. Kim
is visiting his new baby granddaughter, so Bo is all
ours!

There's nothing that cheers me up more than
being with Bo.

He gives us big hugs on the porch and then races into our tiny house. His tail swipes all of Mom's papers off the counter.

"When am I going to learn to put things away before Bo visits?" she says, laughing.

After he's inspected every surface, he stands by the sink.

"Here you go, Bo!" Turtle says, turning on the tap.

Bo is so big that he can drink directly from the faucet.

"Stand back!" I remind Turtle. Bo's drinking can be very sloppy.

Next, Bo races up the stairs to the loft Turtle and I share. When we first got the tiny house, no one thought that a dog as big as Bo could possibly climb the narrow stairs.

But he can!

Unfortunately, he sometimes gets scared climbing down. (Sometimes he even gets halfway and tries to back up.) I have to put one hand on his head and hold out a treat with the other. Then he bravely galumphs down.

When I head up to the loft after dinner, Bo joins me. "I have to read for fifty minutes to reach my goal," I tell him. He seems to understand. He settles down and lets me rest my head on his belly.

Bo is used to kids reading to him. That's what he does all day long in the library at Happy Trails Elementary (except when Mr. Kim takes him on walks or when he comes out to romp with us at recess).

I read silently—I'm faster that way. But Bo must really love stories, because he keeps nudging me with his nose. When I finally give in and read aloud, he sighs happily and lowers his head onto his paws. I can almost hear him say, "Finally!"

"Twig!" Turtle calls from below. "Don't read out loud. I can't solve math problems when you're reading about ghosts who rise up out of the ground."

"But Bo is only happy if I read out loud," I say.

She doesn't respond, so I keep reading:

"'The misty figure walks toward me. It doesn't

35

make a sound.

"'I put out my hand, but still the figure marches forward. And she wasn't alone.'"

"Twig!" Turtle says. "That ghost is messing with my subtraction!"

"Put the headphones on!" I call back.

"Dad's got them. He's listening to music—or something."

"Read silently, Twig," Mom says. She's making a cup of tea, and helping Turtle when she needs it. "Bo will adjust."

"No!" says Turtle, slapping down her pencil. "I changed my mind. I'm coming up. I want to hear what happens next."

"What about your math problems?" Mom says.

"I only have a couple more. I'll do them in the morning."

"Well then," says Mom. "Pajamas and teeth first."

Turtle and I get ready for bed. Determined to add to my reading hours (and maybe beat Matteo after all), I read two more chapters. Unfortunately, Turtle and Bo fall fast asleep (Turtle is breathing hard and Bo is snoring), so I switch to silent reading and keep going.

I can feel my tiredness, but I don't want to stop. I didn't read as much as I should have over the weekend. I push on.

"Lights out, Twigster," Dad says.

I read another page.

"*Twi-ig,*" Mom says.

I read one more paragraph.

"Twig!" Dad says.

"Okay, okay!" I say, reaching up and hitting the light switch.

I sneak a look at the timer on my watch. One hundred and thirty-two minutes!

That's two hours and twelve . . . I yawn. My eyes start to feel sleepy.

Ack!

For some reason Bo wakes and decides to change his sleeping position. This involves lots of stepping on us, but Turtle sleeps through it.

Now my eyes are wide awake again.

I think about the read-a-thon. I wonder if the winning class will take a school bus to the bowling alley. I haven't been in a school bus since we lived in Boston.

Turtle rolls over and begins to talk in her sleep.

"Bubbles not so only don't."

I listen for a moment, but I can't figure out what she's saying.

38

Then, I don't want to, but I can't help it. I think about the soccer game. I can't believe I missed two shots. I recall the groans from the sidelines.

Bo begins to dream. He is not a quiet dreamer. He makes whining noises and his back legs pump as if

he's chasing a truck full of squirrels. Squirrels that are hanging off the back laughing at him.

His legs keep knocking mine. So, I move farther away on my mattress. Now I can feel the edge of the mattress on my back. It's as annoying as mouth noises.

And speaking of mouth noises, I can hear my parents getting ready for bed. First the teeth brushing, then the gargling. Ugh.

I try to think happy thoughts. Happy thoughts like winning the read-a-thon. Happy thoughts like maybe I'm back in the lead with the most reading hours . . .

But then I think of soccer again.

My stomach does a little turn.

"You should have been paying better attention, Twig," I hear in my head.

"You were thinking about the read-a-thon."

"You forgot to watch the kicker."

"You just reacted without thinking."

ZZZZZZZZzzzzzzz

Dad is snoring. And unlike Bo's, his snores involve a lot of snorting.

Everyone is sleeping in this tiny house except me.

The house feels SO CROWDED.

Crowded with sleepers.

Crowded with the sound of the icemaker and the ticktock of the kitchen clock.

Crowded with noises in my head!

CHAPTER 5

"Wake up!" Turtle calls right in my ear.

Here's how you know you're really tired:

• Not even the sounds of a Great Dane howling for his breakfast wakes you up.

• Your sister has to shake you twice before you figure out it's morning.

• You close your eyes again even though you really, really, *really* wanted to read before school.

Somehow, I pull myself out of bed and get dressed. There's yummy yogurt on my granola, but I

43

can hardly lift my spoon.

Fortunately, no matter how tired you are, a Great Dane will get you moving. That, and your little sister saying, "Come on, Twig! We have to get to school!" She hands me Bo's leash since he needs to go too.

Bo has to sniff every pine cone, every fire hydrant, and every wrapper that may have flown from a person's pocket. Then he chases after several talkative crows, and one stripy chipmunk. When he sees a kid he knows from school, he yanks me forward.

It's Matteo, leaning against a tree and reading. It's almost as if he's been waiting for us. If he's tired this morning, his face doesn't show it. His face has the same determined look it does when he's going after a soccer ball.

Bo loves hellos. He wags his whole body. He bounces and twirls. He jumps in the air and knocks

Matteo's book out of his hands.

"Sit, Bo!" Matteo says firmly.

Bo sits.

"Good Pony," he says, and gives him three pats on the head. Lots of kids at school have started calling Bo that since he's almost as tall as a horse.

I bend down to pick up Matteo's book, but Turtle beats me to it.

"Hey, my sister is reading this one too!" she says, handing the book back to him. Sure enough, he's

reading *Ghosts of the Haunted Barn*.

"It's pretty good," Matteo says.

"Yeah, I finished it last night," I tell him.

"You did?" Turtle looks as if I ate the very last slice of Cara's carrot cake.

"I bet Mom or Dad will read you the ending tonight if you ask." I'd offer to read it to her, but *rereading* minutes don't count.

"I can't stop!" Matteo says, holding up the book. "I read during breakfast, and while brushing my teeth, and now while walking to school."

I'm one part jealous that he had the quiet he needed to read all weekend, and two parts determined to finish this week strong.

"How many hours have you read now?" he asks.

I have to admit, it no longer feels as if it's our class competing with the other third- and fourth-grade classes. It feels like Matteo and I are competing with each other. I'm not sure I want to answer. "I don't know," I say, looking down. (It's true, sort of. I haven't added my minutes from last night to my total.)

And that's when I notice something. Something big.

I can tell that Matteo notices at the same time. "Are those your pajamas?" he asks.

Sure enough, I am still wearing my pajama bottoms! I was so sleepy, I forgot to change into pants.

I start to fib . . . to tell him they're flannel leggings,
but Turtle jumps in.

"Yes!" she says. "She decided to be super comfy
at school today because she's going to read every
moment she gets. Right, Twig?"

Turtle is so good at thinking fast. I shoot her a smile.

"Oh," says Matteo, looking deflated. "Well, okay, I better keep reading too." He leans back against the tree and pulls the book to his nose.

I look down at my jams, which have cuddly teddy bears on them. For a moment I thought I was going to have to race home or suffer my most embarrassing day ever. Now, thanks to Turtle, I feel like I have a superpower.

I almost feel sorry for Matteo.

CHAPTER
6

I deliver Bo to the library for his job. He greets
Mr. Lucas, the librarian, and immediately settles
down in his reading corner. Bo is a free spirit
outdoors. But here in the library, due to his special
training, he's all business as a reading dog.

On the way back to my class, I bump into Warren,
who is in the other third-grade class. He's my friend
from Social Skills Club. "Mrs. Hamilton is giving us
a whole hour this morning to read!" he tells me. "No
math or study skills!"

"You lucky ducks!" I say. "Study skills is so boring!" (Even my teacher, Mr. Harbor, would agree, I think.) Maybe there's a way that I can persuade him to give us an hour to read.

Back in my classroom, kids are telling David their reading times and he's recording them in his notebook. I go to my desk and add up my hours and

minutes and then I stand in line to report them.

"Mr. Harbor," my best friend Angela calls from the reading corner. "The bookshelves are empty. I can't find anything new to read."

We're allowed to take as many books home as we want during the read-a-thon. Mr. Harbor looks at the shelves and scratches his head. I bet he didn't realize we'd jump on the chance to borrow armloads of books. "After you've reported your hours," he says, "return the books you've read and we'll see where we are."

Unfortunately, most kids were waiting until they read their whole stack before bringing books back to school. Even after a few kids place books on the shelves, there still aren't many.

"I've still read everything here," Angela says to those of us searching for something new.

"Not having more books is really going to put our class at a disadvantage," Piper says.

"On top of that," I add, "Mrs. Hamilton is giving the other third-grade class an extra hour of reading this morning."

"A whole hour?" asks Matteo. "For all twenty-two kids? That will give their class twenty-two more hours to add to their total!"

Mr. Harbor comes up be-hind us. "A whole extra hour?" he asks me.

I nod.

Mr. Harbor makes a face. I can't tell if it's an "Oh that sneaky Mrs. Hamilton" face or a "Why didn't I think of that?" face? But either way, I can tell his brain wheels are turning.

"Listening to someone else read counts toward hours, right?" he says. "I can read to you from my own collection this morning."

We cheer.

"That gives our class an extra twenty-two hours!" Matteo says.

"And why don't I see if we can get time in the library today?" Mr. Harbor adds, winking. "Then we will have available books and we can add some reading hours." He writes a note to Mr. Lucas, the librarian, and asks David to deliver it for him.

We try to settle down during Morning Meeting, but focusing is nearly impossible. Fortunately, David returns quickly.

"Mr. Lucas says he can give us twenty minutes right after lunch."

Only twenty minutes? The class groans. David grabs a pencil from his desk, turns over the slip of paper in his hand, and calculates. "But that still adds up to an additional seven-point-three hours for our total!" he tells us.

Suddenly winning the read-a-thon is all any of us can think about. "Mr. Harbor, can you read to us for two whole hours today?" Piper asks.

I think for a moment, then raise my hand.

Mr. Harbor gives me a nod.

"Mr. Harbor might get tired from all that reading," I say. "But what if we only had Author's Chair during our Writer's Workshop block? What if we took turns reading our writing to each other during that time? That would count too. Right?"

Mr. Harbor grins at me and I feel as if I just blocked an opposing soccer team's winning goal.

"Great idea! But I suspect your ears would get tired," Mr. Harbor says. "Perhaps we can break the Author's Chair into segments throughout the day. Each of you can have a turn to read before the day is over."

"Yay!" we shout. If Mr. Harbor played soccer, I'd want him on my team.

"But," he says, "there won't be time for compliments and questions."

We love compliments but agree that we'll sacrifice them for the win.

He sends us back to our desks and then takes a moment to choose a read-aloud from his teacher's shelf. I can't wait to see what he picks. (I hope I haven't read it before. I wonder if relistening doesn't count the way rereading doesn't.) Finally, he says, "I think this one is appropriate." He chooses a book about a pig who wants to become a sled dog. "This pig's got persistence," he says. "Just like all of you."

I rest my head on my desk—so so happy that we get to listen to a story early in the morning. The opening of the story is exciting, and Mr. Harbor has a really good reading voice. Still, I can't stop yawning.

How am I going to get the added hours I need tonight to do my very best (and maybe beat Matteo) and still get enough sleep?

My turn to read in the Author's Chair happens right before lunch. I choose to read my story about my little sister winning a toy store contest by accident. Kids seem to like it a lot—maybe because most of them were at the toy store when Turtle won. After lunch we head to the library as promised.

I'm looking forward to seeing Bo again, but he's not on duty. It's his time to have recess with the older kids.

I head right to the Haunted Homes series to see if I can get the next book. Rats! It's checked out. So, I decide to look for an interesting book in nonfiction instead. I find one on trees, which makes me happy. Since my name is Twig, I love all things tree.

As usual, Mr. Lucas invites us all to find a comfortable place in the library to read. There are lots of cool spots. Bo's corner has some comfy beanbags. And there's a couch in the opposite corner. But because we have only twenty minutes to read, every-

one settles into these spots quickly. I look around

the nonfiction area to see if I can find my own

private spot.

That's when I notice that the bottom shelf

beneath PLANTS AND FAUNA is empty. What a cool little cubby! I curl myself onto the shelf. It's fun—like being in the bottom bunk bed. Or in a cool fort. I do my best to open the book (which is a bit on the large size) and begin reading.

I bet you didn't know trees are the superheroes of the natural world is how it begins. I know I'm going to like this book!

I only read a page though when my eyes start to get sleepy—the same way they do at bedtime.

I should sit up, I think.

But I don't want to.

I'll just close my eyes for a moment, and then I'll—

CHAPTER 7

Bo! Licking my face awake!

I sit up and *Bam!* I hit my head on—

That's when I realize that I'm not at home in bed. I'm curled up in a shelf in the school library.

"Twig!" Mr. Lucas says, holding out his hand to help me up. "What are you doing here?"

Mr. Kim is standing behind him. "You wouldn't believe it, Twig," he says. "I came to take Bo with me on my cleaning rounds. But he wouldn't leave the library. Absolutely refused. He pulled me over here."

"Have you been sleeping all this time?" Mr. Lucas asks. "We need to get you back to your classroom."

I wonder how long it's been. "What time is it?" I ask.

"It's nearly dismissal," Mr. Lucas says.

I wrap my arms around Bo's neck. "Good job, Bo!" I say. If it wasn't for the best dog in the world, I might have spent the night in the school library!

I feel silly as I walk back to my classroom with Mr. Lucas at my side.

The kids are stretched out on the carpet, and Mr. Harbor is reading to them again.

"Twig!" he says. He stops reading and comes over to greet me. "I didn't realize you weren't here in class with us."

Mr. Lucas quietly explains that I was asleep in the library.

Mr. Harbor's face turns bright red. "I took the kids straight from the library to art," he says to Mr. Lucas. "Then they went to recess. I'm sorry, Twig," he says, turning to me. "I didn't realize you were missing."

I join the others on the carpet. They're all silent, staring at me. "I accidentally fell asleep in the library," I say, feeling embarrassed. David clasps his hand over his mouth.

"I wondered what happened to you," Angela says.

"I thought maybe it was your time to read with Bo—or that you stayed in the library to help Mr. Lucas with something."

Everyone in the class begins talking at once. They are either telling about weird places where they fell asleep (although most of them were little kids when it happened) or they're brainstorming what they would do if they woke up in the middle of the night and discovered they were trapped in the library.

"Turtle wouldn't have walked home without you," Angela says to me. "She'd make sure you were found."

I smile at Angela. She's right and it makes me happy that I have a sister who wouldn't leave me and a best friend who knows exactly what to say to make me feel better.

Mr. Lucas stays with our class until dismissal

time. Mr. Harbor tells me that he's going to call my parents. He wants them to hear what happened from him.

I wonder what they will say about my big adventure. It's funny. It's one of the most remarkable things that's happened to me since we moved to our tiny house in Happy Trails. And I slept through it all.

CHAPTER 8

Mom and Dad are both standing on the front porch as Turtle and I approach.

"Twig fell asleep in the school library!" Turtle calls out. Either she forgot that I told her that Mr. Harbor called home and Mom and Dad already know, or she doesn't care. She's got to tell someone this news before she explodes.

"So we heard," Mom says as she and Dad give us hugs.

"Come sit down and tell us what happened, Twig," Mom says.

I tell about the added library time and how I crawled into the cozy shelf. How I didn't wake up until Bo (my hero!) licked my face.

"We should have realized that you weren't getting enough sleep!" Dad says, his face turning red the way Mr. Harbor's face had. I realize that my parents must have been just as embarrassed as my teacher was when they learned what had happened.

"It was my fault," I say. "I didn't get enough reading

hours in over the weekend, so I kept on reading past my bedtime last night."

"But, Twig," says Mom, "the only time we left the house this past weekend was when you had soccer. That should have left you plenty of time to read."

"But it's hard reading in a tiny house," I blurt. "It's hard when people are talking and doing flamingo dances—"

"And giving tours," Turtle adds with a little grin.

"Or taking an unexpected shower?" Mom asks.

We all break out laughing.

"I understand what you're saying," Dad says. "Sometimes I want to work on my comics here at home, but I can't concentrate."

"And I'll admit," says Mom, "that a time or two, I've gone to the car to think."

"But we can't be quiet all the time," Turtle says in

an extra-loud voice to make her point.

"No," Dad says, "but perhaps we can have a quiet time each day."

"Like naptime?" says Turtle, making a mean face. She's always hated naptime.

"No," says Mom. "You can do anything you want as long as it's quiet."

"And there's no bouncing!" I add.

Turtle thinks about it for a moment. She likes new and different. And Quiet Time is new and different.

"Teacher's meeting has begun, no more laughing, no more fun," she says. Then she stops. "I can't remember the rest, but can we try it right now?"

"Let's wait until after snack," Dad says. "I want to hear about your day."

"And can we go to the playground first?" I ask. "I've been sleeping all afternoon."

Everyone agrees. Playground first.

We're walking down the sidewalk, halfway there, when Mom suddenly exclaims, "Twig! Are you wearing your pajamas?"

I give her a squinty smile. What can I say?

"Jordan's here!" says Turtle as soon as we've reached the Happy Trails playground. Like most everything in Happy Trails, you can walk to it from our house. There's a fun maze-y playground structure with tunnels and ropes and slides. There's a climbing wall and swings. And there's a little pond with benches around it. The grown-ups like to sit there and look out at the mountains.

Unfortunately, none of my friends seem to be here this afternoon. (I wonder if they are all home, adding to their reading hours.)

"Come on, Twig!" Turtle says. "You can play with us."

"What are you playing?" I ask, following Turtle to the edge of the pond where Jordan is waving us over.

Turtle shrugs. "What are you playing?" she asks Jordan.

"Baby Elephant," Jordan says. "You can play too. And you can be the mama elephant," Jordan says to me. "Turtle and me will be naughty."

I think about this for a moment. I don't want to be a mama elephant. "I'll be a baby elephant too," I say. "We can all be baby elephants."

Jordan thinks about it for a moment and then shrugs. "Okay! Three baby elephants."

We start moving around as if we have long trunks pulling our faces toward the ground.

But then we begin to move into sillier shapes:

baby elephants rolling, baby elephants stuck upside down, baby elephants with feet stuck in the mud, baby elephants tickling each other. The ground is cold, we're getting leaves in our hair, but it's hilarious and we don't care.

I look up at the grown-ups who are talking and don't seem to notice that there are three elephants playing on the edge of a pond in Happy Trails—one of them in her filthy pajamas.

CHAPTER 9

When we get back to the tiny house, we have our first Quiet Time. I change into clean pants and head up the loft to read. Dad sits down and examines a graphic novel. Mom and Turtle sit at the table and work on a puzzle. They agree that it has to be "silent puzzle-making," that they can't say a word.

At first, I can't help peeking down at them. Neither Mom or Turtle are speaking, but I swear I can hear them pointing to puzzle pieces and nodding their heads. And I can hear the puzzle pieces snapping

into place. There's a little part of me that wants to
be down there with them, doing the puzzle. But then
I concentrate on the bird book that Mr. Lucas let me
check out, and before long, I'm lost in my own pages

of feathers and nests and birdsong.

We had agreed that the first Quiet Time should only be a half hour—to get used to it. But no one wants to stop. We are quiet for forty minutes.

I report my weekend number of reading hours as soon as I arrive at school the next day. "Nine hours and five minutes," I say.

"How many hours does our class have?"

David takes a moment to add up the recent figures. "We're at three hundred eight hours and forty-seven minutes."

"How many hours does Matteo have?" I whisper. I don't want Matteo to know that I'm asking.

David scans down his list until he reaches Matteo's name. "In total? Eighty-six hours," he says, "and twenty-eight minutes."

My spirits fall.

"That's good, Twig!" David says. "All those hours are helping our class to get a bowling party."

He's right, of course. Matteo is only helping all of us to win. But it doesn't mean I feel better.

Fortunately, Mr. Harbor has borrowed lots of books from the Happy Trails library to put on our shelves. He reads to us for an hour and allows us to have forty minutes of independent reading time.

At home, Turtle reminds us that it's Quiet Time right after we have our snack. We all agree. This is our new favorite thing!

Dad sits at the table and adds color to his comic-book pages. Mom reads on the couch. Turtle curls up on the floor and listens to an audiobook on her headphones. Every now and then, she laughs—she can't help it—but then goes back to listening again. (I wish I had thought to curl up with her. I could have gotten more hours that way!) In the old days, I would have called down, "What's so funny?" but none of us want to burst the quiet bubble.

Today, Quiet Time lasts for more than an hour!

The next day is different. Wednesdays are often half days at school since our teachers need learning time too. Mr. Harbor tells us that there's no time for read-aloud or for independent reading. (*Boo!* we mouth to one another.)

After school I have a soccer match, so no Quiet Time either.

Matteo and I are the first kids to arrive at the soccer field. I sit next to him on the bench and tie on my new cleats.

"How much—"

I brace myself. I know what he's going to say.

How much did you read last night?

But instead he says, "How much of a difference do your cleats make?"

His question surprises me. I look down and notice he's wearing sneakers.

I thought about saying *They make a difference! I can really grip the ground*, but I stop myself. Truth is, I don't really know if they made a difference in the last game or not.

"I'm not sure," I tell him. "I was so nervous about being goalkeeper, I didn't notice."

He nods. "I'm not very good at soccer," he says. "My parents don't want to invest in cleats until they know I'm going to stick with it."

"You're not bad!" I say, which is true. "You intercepted the ball last game!"

His face brightens, like he's happy I noticed. "I didn't hold it very long," he says.

"But you were really in there."

He smiles because both of us know that in soccer, that's something.

And that's when Coach Ruby says she'd like to have me start as goalkeeper again.

"Really?" I ask. I'm shocked.

"Glove up," she tells me. "And make sure you have wrist bands to hold those gloves on tight."

I can't believe she's giving me another chance so soon.

I exchange surprised looks with Matteo, then head out onto the field and practice jumping high into the air.

The coin toss hasn't even happened be-fore I start to hear all the voices in my head again. The voices that tell me to focus, that remind me of rules . . .

The other team gets the ball first. They start dribbling in my direction.

Even though my eye is on the ball, spectators

start shouting things to me.

I talk to myself. "Remember, Twig. Hands like a *W* if the ball's high in the air, hands like an *M* if the ball's low to the ground."

And then, as the ball starts speeding in my direction, I tell all those voices to STOP!

"It's Quiet Time!" I say.

I center myself.

I focus.

I don't even hear the voices on the sidelines anymore. It's just me and the game, and I'm in it.

All the way to our win.

CHAPTER 10

By Thursday afternoon, Quiet Time in our tiny house feels regular.

Dad purchased another set of headphones. He and Turtle are watching a movie together. Mom is sitting at the counter, answering e-mails.

And I am reading.

I'm sort of getting sick of reading, to be honest (and jealous of Turtle). Before this read-a-thon, it was one of my favorite things to do. Right up there with eating one of Cara's cupcakes. But I suppose if

I had to eat one hundred of Cara's cupcakes, I'd get tired of those too.

Right now, everyone in my family has extreme focus. I've read for over an hour and I'm ready to do something else. But I don't want to interrupt the others. Especially when I was the one who wanted this quiet time so badly.

So, I pull out my little fragile skunks and begin playing a game on my sleeping bag. I wish Turtle was available to play with me.

I listen to the *click-clack* of Mom's laptop keys. It sort of makes me lonely.

I imagine myself living all alone in this loft . . . somewhere deep in the wilderness.

I miss the sound of my father jumping down from his loft ladder and saying, "Ugh. I've got to lose some weight."

I miss the sound of my sister trying to blow bubbles.

I miss the sound of my mother telling Bo that he's not allowed to put his front paws on the counter.

And the sound of her singing.

All of a sudden, my heart hurts.

I decide to go downstairs. Maybe my presence will make others want to move, want to speak again. I walk into the kitchen, but no one stirs!

I notice that before Mom got on her laptop, she prepared food for tacos. There are black beans simmering on the stove and little bowls of chopped tomatoes and cheese—and jalapeno peppers for Dad. The taco shells are on a cookie sheet, waiting to go into the oven. Surely it must be time to finish this meal up!

I tiptoe over to Mom and whisper (which is probably against the rules), "Can I put the taco shells in the oven?"

She looks up at the clock, and then nods in a sort of distracted way.

"Yay!" I put on the oven mitts and carefully slide the taco shells onto the top shelf just like Mom showed me the last time we made cookies.

I'm looking out the window, waiting for the delicious smell of taco shells to make everyone stop what they're doing and come into the kitchen, when suddenly, smoke starts seeping out of the oven!

"Mom!"

She jumps up, grabs a mitt and opens the door.

Black smoke billows out and sets off the smoke detector.

SCRRRREEEEEAAACH!

It's so loud that Dad and Turtle pull off their headphones and come running.

Dad grabs the fire extinguisher and gets ready to attack the oven.

Mom leads Turtle and me out of the house while he sprays.

"I'm so sorry!" I say to Mom. "I didn't know they would catch on fire!"

"No worries," she says. "Things in the oven catch fire sometimes. Dad will take care of it."

Apparently, our smoke detector automatically sends a message to the fire department. It only takes minutes for a truck to arrive. Two firefighters rush past me and Turtle and into the house.

"Is the house going to burn down?" Turtle asks.

Mom gives us a comforting smile. "No," she says, putting her arms around us both. "I bet that little fire is out already."

Mr. Bryant, the owner of Sudsy's Laundromat, comes running outside to see what's happening. So do several of his customers. And Cara. And Piper and her family who live down the street. And Mrs. Wallaby who owns the toy store. And Georgia from the Vintage Store. And Matteo's family, who were looking for cleats at the Vintage Store.

It's that time of day when shops are closing and people are on their way home. But now we are all standing outside the tiny house in the almost-dark waiting to see what will happen next.

Snow.

That's what happens next. Big lovely snowflakes
float down past the streetlights and land on our
faces.

It's the first snow of the season and it feels

magical.

Dad and the firefighters come out of the house

together. Laughing.

Laughing?

Dad thanks the firefighters and then he says hello

to everyone standing in the street. "Come inside," he

says. "Come on inside and I'll tell you a funny thing

that happened."

Have I said that our house is tiny? It is very tiny. But for some reason, everyone decides that they'd love to come inside and hear Dad's story. There are people sitting on the stairs, and on the couch, and on the floor. People standing in the kitchen take some rags from Mr. Bryant and begin wiping all the white powder that came from the fire extinguisher off the cupboards and the counter and the floor.

And before Dad can start his story, Cara slips out and brings back all of her days' leftovers to share.

"Is this your photograph?" someone asks Mom as they stare at a picture of us girls on a wall.

"And are these your comics?" they ask Dad.

"These carrot chips are delicious," people tell Cara.

Then Mrs. Wallaby says to Dad, "Tell us your story!"

And so, Dad tells us how he blasted the flame in the oven with the spray from the fire extinguisher, but it refused to go out! No matter how much he sprayed, the flame stayed lit.

"Finally," he says, "one of the firefighters told me to stand back and wait."

Wait? Wait for what?

The whole room is quiet.

"I waited until the powder settled, and that's when I saw that it was the oven light that I was trying to put out."

The whole room burst into laughter.

And the snow fell.

And no one—especially me—wished for quiet.

CHAPTER 11

I couldn't wait to get to school the next day. Not only was Mrs. Martinez, the principal, going to announce the winner of the read-a-thon, but I had the best story in the world to tell during Writer's Workshop. I couldn't wait to get it written so I could read it in Author's Chair.

We gave our reading hours to David, who tallied them up. Then Mr. Harbor wrote our hours on a slip of paper, and David got the honor of taking it to the office.

"How many hours did you read?" Matteo asks me as I return the books I borrowed.

I tell him. "How about you?" I ask.

He read more. But before I can say anything, he says, "At first I didn't even want to do the read-a-thon."

"You didn't? How come?"

"I like to read, but I didn't want to spend all my time reading unless we had a real chance of winning."

"What convinced you?"

"You!"

"Me?"

"Yes. You were so excited. Everyone knows how much you love reading. And that you're good at it. I figured if I tried to keep up with you, we'd have a really good shot. So I did."

"Me too," says Angela. "Tried to keep up with you, that is."

I feel like I'm glowing. I didn't read the most, but I played my part. And it feels good.

At the end of the day, Mrs. Martinez's voice comes over the intercom.

"First of all, I want all of the third- and fourth-graders at Happy Trails Elementary to know how proud we are! You read more hours during this read-a-thon than in any other year!"

"Hooray!" shouts everyone in our room. We can hear cheers from Mrs. Hamilton's room across the hall too.

"And now, to announce the winning class in this year's read-a-thon."

I bite my lip and look around the room. Everyone

looks as if they're holding their breath.

"Congratulations to . . . Mr. Harbor's third-grade class!" she says. "They read three hundred ninety-five hours and six minutes!"

"Woot woot!" We wag our bodies. We bounce and twirl. We jump in the air.

Matteo gives me a high five.

"I'm lousy at bowling," I tell him.

"Doesn't matter," he says.

"Right," I say. "As long as we're in the game."

Don't miss more
Twig and Turtle Adventures in

CHAPTER 1

Today is going to be a good day.

No, not just a *good* day. A great day.

No, not just a *great* day. A stupendous day!

I decide to choose ribbons for my sneaker laces to celebrate three things:

- It's my turn to read to Bo, the school reading dog.

- Angela (my best friend) and I are going to be on the committee to plan my class's Autumn Harvest Party. Our first meeting is today.

• Mom and Dad are going on a parents' vacation (okay, not so great), but Grandma is coming to stay in our tiny house! And she's going to be with us a whole week!

I'm almost ready to leave for school when I suddenly remember my bracelet. I race back upstairs and retrieve it from my shelf. Angela braided it for me. One strand of the braid is a yellow shoelace, one is a piece of twine, and one is a blue ribbon—just like the materials I thread in my sneakers depending on my moods. "No matter what you decide to lace your sneakers with, your bracelet will match!" she said when she gave it to me.

Like I said, she's my very, very best friend.

"Time for hugs!" Mom says as Turtle and I hoist our backpacks on.

"Text Grandma some vacation cartoons!" Turtle

tells Dad, who is a comic book artist.

"Text lots of pictures!" I tell Mom, who is a pho-tographer.

"We will! We will!" they say. "And we'll video call often."

When we finally get out the door, I have a little tear growing in the corner of my left eye. But then I remind myself that Grandma will be there when we get home.

"I wonder what Grandma will bring this time?" Turtle says, as the crossing guard waves us across the street.

ABOUT THE AUTHOR

JENNIFER RICHARD JACOBSON is the award-winning author of many books for children and young adults, including the Andy Shane early-reader series and her most recent book, *The Dollar Kids*. A graduate of Harvard Graduate School of Education, when not writing, Jennifer provides trainings in Writer's Workshop for teachers. Jennifer lives in Maine with her husband and dog.